T0193772

BARK AT THE
THUNDER

Written and Illustrated by
CAROL A. WOLF

Order this book online at www.trafford.com
or email orders@trafford.com

Most Trafford titles are also available at major online book retailers.

 www.trafford.com

North America & international
toll-free: 844 688 6899 (USA & Canada)
fax: 812 355 4082

Our mission is to efficiently provide the world's finest, most comprehensive book publishing service, enabling every author to experience success. To find out how to publish your book, your way, and have it available worldwide, visit us online at www.trafford.com

ISBN: 978-1-6987-0700-6 (sc)
ISBN: 978-1-6987-0701-3 (e)

Library of Congress Control Number: 2021908262

Print information available on the last page.

Trafford rev. 04/24/2021

DEDICATION

This book is dedicated to my sweet Casey and to her recently departed and much-loved friend Marley, whose actions inspired this story. It is also dedicated to all the family and friends who have encouraged me, and to my Savior Jesus, to whom I give all credit for any talent I have.

Marley and Casey lived next door to each other and were very good friends. They went on walks together and even shared treats.

But there was one big difference. Marley was not afraid of thunder. Casey was. The thunder was loud and invisible and scary and no one knew where it came from. It just *was*.

Sometimes it came in a low rumble that could barely be heard. But the dogs heard it. The dogs knew. Other times it was a sudden loud CRACK!

Marley and Casey were sitting on the porch when the thunder rumbled softly. Casey edged over to her person, Carol. Marley stood up.

It rumbled again, louder. Casey leaned hard against Carol, as Carol spoke to her softly and stroked her. It didn't help much. She was still afraid. Marley ran out into the yard and barked loudly.

"How can you do that?" shuddered Casey.

"Do what?" panted Marley in excitement as he scrambled back onto the porch.

"Run out there and bark when it thunders," she shuddered again.

"I'm barking *at* the thunder," Marley insisted." I'm not just making noise. I'm talking to it."

"I don't understand," replied Casey. "What's the difference?"

"What do you do when it thunders?" asked Marley.

"I hug up to Carol as closely as I can," answered Casey.

"Why?"

"Because it's scary, and I know she'll protect me."

"And she does," said Marley, "just like Mary would if I went to her. But what happens the next time it thunders?"

"The same thing. I get scared and Carol protects me."

"So, you're afraid every time it thunders? *Every single time*?"

"Well, yes. Aren't you?"

"Absolutely not! All over the Bible God says *do not fear*. He never says it's okay to be afraid."

"But how can you *not* be afraid?"

"By having faith. By believing Him and doing what he says. By speaking to the thunder. In Mark 11: 22-24, he tells us to speak to the mountain. He doesn't say talk about it or be afraid of it. He says *speak* to it. So, if we believe his Word and speak to the thunder, with authority, it must obey. Have you noticed what happens when I bark at the thunder?" Marley continued.

"Well, it goes away. Eventually."

"Right! Now sometimes the thunder tries harder and keeps going. When that happens, I go right back out there again and bark as often and as long as I need to. It always quits."

"That's true," said Casey, who was often so afraid that she didn't notice when the thunder stopped.

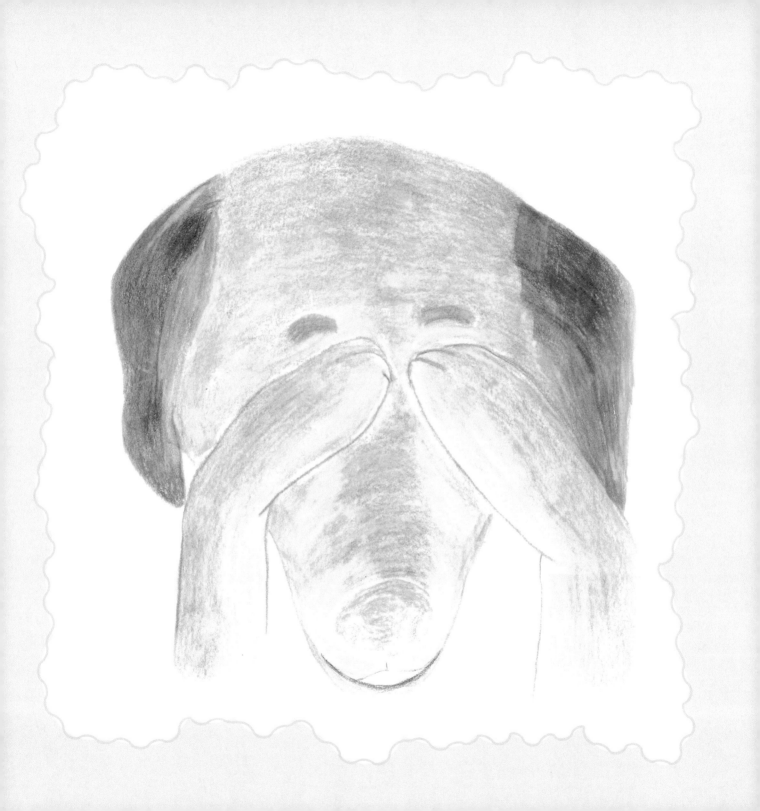

"But what about when the thunder comes back tomorrow or next week? It always does."

"Yes. And you're always afraid of it."

"True."

"And I am always *not* afraid of it," said Marley. You want to know why? Because as big and loud and mysterious as thunder is, we have God on our side, and He is bigger and more powerful than anything. He doesn't lie, and He wouldn't tell me to do something that I couldn't do with Him."

"I bark at the thunder because God said to. I'm not afraid because He is *in* me. The thunder obeys because I have faith and use God's Word against it."

"And when it comes back? Then what?" asked Casey, still unsure.

"Then I do it again!" replied Marley.

"It might be nice to not be afraid of it all the time," said Casey. "It's no fun shaking so much when it thunders."

"Exactly!"

A few days later the dogs were on the porch when they heard a low rumble of thunder. Marley's eyes twinkled as he said to Casey, "Come on kid, you can do this."

"Are you sure?" she asked.

"Greater is He that is in you...."

Taking a deep breath, she said, "Okay, God, let's do this."

The next rumble was louder. Marley shot off the porch like a rocket, and barked, "Go away thunder! You have no right to be here!"

Caught up in the excitement, Casey followed. "Go away thunder! You have no power here!"

Both dogs ran back to the porch, and then dashed into the yard again for the next big boom, barking excitedly, shouting at the thunder.

Some time later the thunder quit. The dogs lay side by side on the porch, panting in excitement.

Casey had discovered she wasn't afraid when she trusted God.

Printed in the United States
by Baker & Taylor Publisher Services